DISCOVER AFRICA

SPANISH Bilingual EDITION

Elando Común

Common Eland

Cobra Egipcia

Egyptian Cobra

Elefante

Elephant

Cabra

Female Goat

Flamingo

Flamingo

Antílope Orix

Gemsbok Antelope

Serpiente Picuda Enana

Dwarf Beaked Snake

Jirafa Madre y el Bebé

Giraffe Mother and Baby

Jirafas

Giraffes

Erizo

Hedgehog

Hipopótamo

Hippopotamus

Hiena

Hyena

Kudu

Kudu

Lechwes

Lechwe

Lémur

Lemur

Familia del León

Lion Family

Avestruz

Ostrich

Rinoceronte con el Becerro

Rhino with Calf

Rinoceronte

Rhinoceros

Rana de Arena

Sand Frog

Antílope

Waterbuck

Toro Watusi

Watusi Bull

Rinoceronte Blanco

White Rhino

Cebra

Zebra

Make Sure to Check Out the Other Discover Series Books from Xist Publishing:

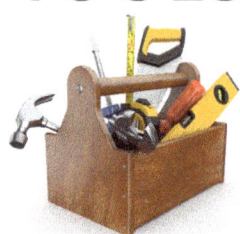

- DISCOVER SERIES: OCEAN Animals
- DISCOVER SERIES: PUPPIES
- DISCOVER SERIES: HORSES
- DISCOVER SERIES: FOSSILS
- DISCOVER SERIES: BUGS
- DISCOVER SERIES: BABY THINGS
- DISCOVER SERIES: TOOLS
- DISCOVER SERIES: MILITARY Book 1
- DISCOVER SERIES: TRANSPORTATION
- DISCOVER SERIES: FIREFIGHTER

Published in the United States by Xist Publishing
www.xistpublishing.com
PO Box 61593 Irvine, CA 92602

© 2017 First Bilingual Edition by Xist Publishing
Spanish Translation by Victor Santana
All rights reserved
No portion of this book may be reproduced without express permission of the publisher
All images licensed from Fotolia

ISBN: 978-1-53240-222-7 EISBN 978-1-53240-127-5

xist Publishing